THE WIZARD OF OZ

In Kansas, there are no witches or wizards. But there *are* cyclones, and one day a cyclone blows Dorothy's house, with Dorothy and her dog Toto in it, to a country called Oz. And in Oz there are four witches and a very famous wizard—the Wizard of Oz.

Dorothy wants to go home to Kansas, but she doesn't know how to get there. She needs help. "Go to the Emerald City," the Witch of the North tells her, "and ask the Wizard of Oz to help you."

Then Dorothy meets the Scarecrow, the Tin Man, and the Cowardly Lion, but they need help too. So they all take the yellow brick road to the Emerald City. But what are they going to find there? Who—or what—*is* the famous Wizard of Oz?

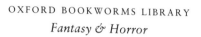

OXFORD BOOKWORMS LIBRARY
Fantasy & Horror

The Wizard of Oz

Stage 1 (400 headwords)

Series Editor: Jennifer Bassett
Founder Editor: Tricia Hedge
Activities Editors: Jennifer Bassett and Alison Baxter

American Edition: Daphne Mackey, University of Washington

L. FRANK BAUM

The Wizard of Oz

Retold by
Rosemary Border

Illustrated by
Gillian McLean

OXFORD UNIVERSITY PRESS

OXFORD

UNIVERSITY PRESS

Great Clarendon Street, Oxford OX2 6DP

Oxford University Press is a department of the University of Oxford.
It furthers the University's objective of excellence in research, scholarship,
and education by publishing worldwide in

Oxford New York

Auckland Cape Town Dar es Salaam Hong Kong Karachi
Kuala Lumpur Madrid Melbourne Mexico City Nairobi
New Delhi Shanghai Taipei Toronto

With offices in

Argentina Austria Brazil Chile Czech Republic France Greece
Guatemala Hungary Italy Japan Poland Portugal Singapore
South Korea Switzerland Thailand Turkey Ukraine Vietnam

OXFORD and OXFORD ENGLISH are registered trade marks of
Oxford University Press in the UK and in certain other countries

ISBN 978 0 19 423745 1

Printed in China

CONTENTS

1

THE CYCLONE

Dorothy lived in a small house in Kansas, with Uncle Henry, Aunt Em, and a little black dog called Toto.

There were no trees and no hills in Kansas, and it was often very windy. Sometimes the wind came very fast and very suddenly. That was a cyclone, and it could blow trees, people, and buildings away. There were cellars under all the houses. And when a cyclone came, people went down into their cellars and stayed there.

A cyclone could blow trees, people, and buildings away.

One day Uncle Henry came out and looked up at the sky. Then he ran quickly back into the house.

"There's a cyclone coming," he called to Aunt Em and Dorothy. "We have to go down into the cellar!"

They ran to the door of the cellar, but Toto was afraid, and he ran under the bed. Dorothy ran after him.

"Quick!" shouted Aunt Em from the cellar. "Leave the dog and come down into the cellar!"

Dorothy picked up Toto and ran to the cellar door. But before she got there, the cyclone hit the house.

And then a very strange thing happened.

The house moved, and then it went slowly up, up, up into the sky. Aunt Em and Uncle Henry were down in the cellar under the ground, but the house, Dorothy, and Toto went up to the top of the cyclone. Dorothy looked through the open cellar door and saw hills and houses, a long way down. She closed the cellar door quickly.

The wind blew the house along for many hours. At first Dorothy was afraid.

"But we can't do anything about it," she said to Toto. "So let's wait and see." And after two or three hours, she and Toto went to sleep.

When Dorothy opened her eyes again, the house was on the ground, and everything was quiet. She picked up Toto, opened the door, and went out. They saw tall trees, beautiful flowers, and little houses with blue doors.

The house went slowly up, up, up into the sky.

3

"Thank you, thank you!" said the woman.

Dorothy gave a little cry. "This isn't Kansas, Toto! And who are these people?"

There were three very short men in blue hats, coats and trousers, and a little old woman in a beautiful white dress. The woman walked up to Dorothy and said, "Thank you, thank you! Now the people are free!"

"Why are you thanking me?" Dorothy asked.

"You killed the Witch of the East," said the woman. "She was a bad witch, and her people, the Munchkins, were very afraid of her. Now she is dead, and we and the Munchkins want to thank you."

The little old woman and the three little men all smiled happily at Dorothy, but Dorothy did not understand.

"But I didn't kill anybody!" she said.

"Your house fell on the Witch," laughed the little woman. "Look! You can see her feet!"

Dorothy looked and saw two feet with red shoes under the house. Suddenly, one of the Munchkins gave a shout. "Look! Her feet are disappearing in the hot sun."

A second later, there were only the red shoes.

"Good," said the little woman. She picked up the shoes and gave them to Dorothy. "They're your shoes now. You must wear them because a witch's shoes can sometimes do wonderful things."

"Thank you," said Dorothy. "But who are you? Are you a Munchkin?"

"No, but I'm their friend. I'm the Witch of the North, and I came to see the dead Witch of the East. But don't be afraid—I'm a good witch."

"Look! Her feet are disappearing!"

5

"But Aunt Em says there aren't any witches."

"Oh yes, there are!" said the Witch. "Here in the country of Oz we have four witches. The witches of the North and the South are good witches, but those of the East and the West are bad witches. Now the Witch of the East is dead, so there is only one bad witch. We have a famous wizard, too. We call him the Wizard of Oz, and he lives in the Emerald City. How many witches and wizards do you have in your country?"

"We don't have any," said Dorothy. Suddenly she remembered Aunt Em and Uncle Henry. "How can I get back home to Kansas?" she asked.

"Where is Kansas?" asked the good Witch. "I don't know a country called Kansas, so I can't tell you the way."

Dorothy began to cry. "Oh dear! What can I do?"

"Please don't cry!" said the Witch. "Go and see the Wizard of Oz. He's a good wizard, and perhaps he can help you. It's a long way, and you have to walk there. I can't go with you, but I can give you my kiss."

She gave Dorothy a little kiss. It looked like a small red flower on Dorothy's face.

"Now nothing can hurt you," she said. "Look—there is the road to the Emerald City. It is made of yellow bricks, so you can't lose your way … Goodbye."

"Goodbye!" said the three little Munchkins.

In the house Dorothy found some bread and some apples, and she put them all in a bag. Then she put on her blue and white dress. "Now I look nice," she said. She looked down at her old shoes. Then she remembered the bad Witch's red shoes and put them on.

She picked up her bag of food. "Come on, Toto!" she called. "We're going to find the Wizard of Oz."

The Witch gave Dorothy a little kiss.

7

2

THE YELLOW BRICK ROAD

Dorothy and Toto walked along the yellow brick road for a long time. When they were tired, they stopped in a field by the road. Not far away, there was a scarecrow, and Dorothy and Toto walked across to look at it.

"Good day," said the Scarecrow.

"Oh!" said Dorothy. "You can speak!"

"Of course I can speak," said the Scarecrow. "But I can't move, up here on this pole … I'd like to get down. Can you help me?"

Carefully, Dorothy took the Scarecrow off his pole.

"Thank you very much," said the Scarecrow. He moved his arms and legs, and straw went everywhere. "Who are you?" he asked. "And where are you going?"

"I'm Dorothy, and I'm going to the Emerald City. I want to go home to Kansas, but I don't know the way. I'm going to ask the Wizard of Oz for help."

"Where is the Emerald City?" asked the Scarecrow. "And who is the Wizard of Oz? I don't know anything, you see, because I have no brains in my head—only straw."

"Oh dear!" said Dorothy. "I'm very sorry."

"I would very much like to have some brains," the

*The Scarecrow moved his arms and legs,
and straw went everywhere.*

Scarecrow said. "Can I go to the Emerald City with you?
Perhaps the Wizard of Oz can give me some brains.
What do you think?"

"I don't know," said Dorothy. "But yes, please come
with me. He's a famous wizard, so perhaps he can help
you." She felt very sorry for the Scarecrow. "Don't be
afraid of Toto," she said. "He never hurts people."

"I am afraid of fire."

"Nothing can hurt me," said the Scarecrow. "I'm not afraid of anything … Well, that's not true. I *am* afraid of fire, of course."

Dorothy walked along the road with her new friend. Soon she began to feel hungry, so she sat down, and she and Toto ate some bread and apples. "Would you like some, Scarecrow?" said Dorothy.

"No, thank you," said the Scarecrow. "I don't need to eat or drink. You can't eat when you're made of straw … Now, tell me about your home."

So Dorothy told him about Kansas, Uncle Henry, Aunt Em, and the cyclone.

"But why do you want to leave this beautiful country?" asked the Scarecrow. "Kansas, you say, has no trees, no green hills, and no gardens. I don't understand."

"That's because you have no brains," said Dorothy. "Kansas is my home. We say, 'East, west—home's best,' and it's true. I want to go home."

10

They walked along the road for some hours, and then it got dark. Dorothy was tired, and soon the Scarecrow saw a little house behind some trees. There was nobody there, so they went in. Dorothy and Toto slept, but the Scarecrow just stood all night with his eyes open.

"Scarecrows don't sleep," he said.

*   *   *

In the morning Dorothy looked for water.

"Why do you want water?" asked the Scarecrow.

"Toto and I are thirsty. And I need to wash."

"I'm sorry for you," said the Scarecrow. "You need a lot of things! But *you* have brains, and *you* can think, and that's wonderful."

They found some water, and Dorothy washed. Then she and Toto ate some bread. Suddenly, they heard a shout from the trees near the house, and they all ran out of the house to look.

They found some water, and Dorothy washed.

11

They saw a man by a big tree, with an ax in his hand. He was made of tin. He stood very still and shouted "Help!" again and again.

"What can I do for you?" asked Dorothy.

"I can't move," said the Tin Man. "Please oil me. There's an oil can in my house."

At once Dorothy ran back to the house and found the oil can. Then she came back and, with the Scarecrow's help, she carefully oiled the Tin Man. Slowly, he began to move, first his head, and then his arms and legs.

"Thank you," he said. "I feel better now." He put down his ax. "I went out in the rain, you see, and water is very bad for a tin body. I was there for a long time, and nobody came to help me."

"We stopped at your house for the night," Dorothy said, "and we heard your shout this morning."

"Where are you going?" asked the Tin Man.

So Dorothy told him about the Wizard of Oz. "I want to go back to Kansas, and the Scarecrow wants some brains," she said.

The Tin Man was very interested. "Can the Wizard give me a heart, do you think? I have no heart, so I can't love or feel ... I would very much like to have a heart."

"Come with us," said the Scarecrow.

"Yes," said Dorothy. "And then you can ask the Wizard for help, too."

Dorothy carefully oiled the Tin Man.

So they all walked along the yellow brick road. There were many tall trees next to the road, and sometimes the three friends heard noises from animals behind the trees. Dorothy did not like these noises very much.

"How far is it to the Emerald City?" she asked the Tin Man. "Do you know?"

"It's a long way, I think," said the Tin Man. "And we must be careful because—"

But just then a big lion suddenly ran out from the trees, into the road. It opened its mouth—it had long yellow teeth—and began to run after Toto.

Dorothy was afraid for Toto. She ran up to the lion and hit it on the nose with her bag. "Don't hurt my dog!" she cried angrily. "He's smaller than you!"

Dorothy hit the lion on the nose with her bag.

"I didn't hurt him," said the Lion. "Don't hit me again—please!"

"Why—you're afraid!" said Dorothy. "Be quiet, Toto, he isn't going to hurt you. He's more afraid than you are. He's just a big coward."

"It's true," said the Lion. "I *am* a coward. Everyone thinks lions are brave. I make a lot of noise, but I'm not brave. I'm just a coward." And the Cowardly Lion began to cry.

Then Dorothy told him about the Wizard of Oz. "Come with us to the Emerald City," she said. "I want to go back to Kansas, the Scarecrow wants some brains, and the Tin Man wants a heart. Perhaps the Wizard of Oz can make you brave."

"Oh, thank you!" said the Lion. "I would very much like to be brave."

And so the Cowardly Lion came with them. At first Toto was afraid of him, but very soon he and the Lion were good friends.

That night Dorothy and Toto slept under a big tree next to the Cowardly Lion's big, warm body. In the morning they ate the last of their bread.

"Oh dear!" said Dorothy. "What are we going to eat for dinner?"

"I can kill an animal for you," said the Cowardly Lion.

"Oh no—please don't kill anything!" the Tin Man said.

He began to cry. "We don't want to hurt any animals. I haven't got a heart, but I feel sorry for them."

Dorothy quickly got out the oil can and oiled his face.

"Don't cry," she said. "You know water is bad for you."

They walked along the yellow road, and after an hour or two they came to a big river.

"Oh no!" said Dorothy. "How can we get across?"

The Lion looked down at the river. "I'm very afraid of falling," he said, "but I think I can jump across."

"Good!" said the Scarecrow at once. "You can carry us on your back, one at a time."

So the Cowardly Lion jumped across the river, first

So the Cowardly Lion jumped across the river.

The Tin Man cut down the tree with his ax.

with the Scarecrow on his back, then with Dorothy and Toto, and last with the Tin Man.

But soon they came to a second river. This one was very big, and the Lion could not jump across it. The Scarecrow thought for a minute.

"Look," he said. "There's a tall tree next to the river. The Tin Man can cut it down with his ax. And when the tree falls across the river, we can walk across the tree."

"Very good," said the Lion. "For somebody with straw in their head and not brains."

So the Tin Man cut down the tree with his ax, and soon they were all across that river, too.

3

THE EMERALD CITY

It was a long day. The yellow brick road went past fields, through trees, up hills, and down hills. In the evening they began to see small green houses by the road. Sometimes little people in green clothes came out and looked at the friends. But they did not come near them because they were afraid of the Cowardly Lion.

"Everything here is green. Perhaps we're near the Emerald City," said Dorothy. "Toto and I are hungry. Let's stop at the next house."

A little woman opened the door, and Dorothy said, "Please can we stay the night in your house?" The little woman looked at the Lion, and Dorothy said quickly, "The Lion is my friend, and he never hurts anybody."

"All right," the little woman said. "You can all come in." She put a wonderful dinner on the table. Dorothy and Toto ate a lot of it, and the Lion ate some of it. But the Scarecrow and the Tin Man ate nothing.

"Where are you all going?" asked the little woman.

"To the Emerald City," said Dorothy. "We want to see the Wizard of Oz."

"That's not easy," said the woman. "The Wizard never goes out of his house, and nobody sees his face."

"Is the Wizard a man?" asked the Scarecrow.

"Nobody knows," said the woman. "He's a wizard, so he might be a man, or an animal—or anything!"

"How strange!" said Dorothy. "But we need his help, so we *must* see him."

The next day they thanked the woman, left the house, and began walking again. Soon they saw a beautiful city in front of them—it was the Emerald City at last.

It was the Emerald City at last.

19

The friends went up the yellow brick road to a big green door and stopped. Slowly, the door opened, and a little man in green clothes stood there.

"We want to see the Wizard, please," said Dorothy.

"Nobody sees the Wizard," he said. "He is a very good and very famous Wizard, but nobody can see him."

"We *must* see him," said Dorothy. "Please ask him."

"All right," said the green man. "I can take you to his house. But first, you must all put glasses on." He opened a big box. In it were lots of glasses. "You must wear your glasses all the time," he said. "Everybody in the city must wear glasses. The Wizard says this."

So they all put on glasses. The green man put on some glasses too, and then he took them through the Emerald City. Everything in the city was green—men, women, children, houses, shops, streets …

The green man took them to a very big house, and they went into a long green room. "Wait here," he said. After a short time he came back.

"You can see the Wizard," he said. "But you must go to him one by one. He wants to see the little girl first."

Then he went away, and a green girl came in. She took Dorothy to a tall green door.

"The Wizard is in there," said the green girl. "He's waiting for you."

Dorothy went in. On a green chair was a very, very big

"Everybody in the city must wear glasses," said the green man.

head. There was no body, or arms, or legs—only a head.
Its mouth opened, and the Head said: "I am Oz. Who are
you, and what do you want?"

"I am Dorothy," said the child bravely.

"Where did you get those red shoes?"

"From the bad Witch of the East," said Dorothy. "My house fell on her and killed her."

"What is that thing on your face?"

"A kiss. The good Witch of the North kissed me," said Dorothy. "I need help, and she told me about you."

"And what do you want?"

On a green chair was a very, very big head.

"I want to go home to Kansas," answered Dorothy, "but I don't know the way. Please help me to get home."

The big eyes opened and closed, opened and closed. Then the mouth opened, and the Head spoke again. "Well," it said, "perhaps I can help you. But first, *you* must do something for *me.*"

"What do you want me to do?" asked Dorothy.

"Kill the bad Witch of the West."

"But I don't want to kill anybody!" said Dorothy.

"You killed her sister. And you are wearing her shoes. Go now, and kill the Witch of the West."

The little girl began to cry. "But how can I kill the Witch?" she said. The big eyes opened and looked at her, but the Head did not answer. Dorothy went away, and then her friends went into the Wizard's room—first the Scarecrow, then the Tin Man, and last the Lion.

Later, they all met in the long green room and talked. Dorothy told her friends about the Head.

"That's interesting," said the Scarecrow. "I didn't see a Head; I saw a beautiful woman. I asked her for some brains and she said, 'Yes, but first you must help Dorothy to kill the Witch of the West.'"

"I saw a big animal with two heads," said the Tin Man. "I asked for a heart. The animal said, 'I can give you a heart; but first you must help Dorothy to kill the Witch of the West.' What did you see, Lion?"

"I saw a ball of fire," said the Cowardly Lion.

"I saw a ball of fire," said the Cowardly Lion. "I said, 'I'm a coward; please make me brave.' And the fire said, 'When the Witch of the West is dead, I can help you. But not before.' I was angry then," said the Lion, "but the ball of fire got bigger and bigger, so I ran away."

"Oh, what are we going to do?" said Dorothy.

"Well," said the Scarecrow. "We must find the Witch of the West, and then we must kill her."

4

THE WITCH AND THE MONKEYS

The next morning they left the Emerald City. The green man took away their glasses and told them the way to the Witch's house. "Everybody is afraid of the Witch of the West," he said. "So be careful!"

The friends walked for a long time. The road was bad, and there were no houses, no fields, and no trees.

Now the Witch of the West had a magic eye, and it could see everything. She saw the friends on the road, and she was angry. She put on her tall black hat and shouted, "Magic Monkeys—come!"

"Magic Monkeys—come!"

In a second forty monkeys arrived at her tall house. "What do you want?" they asked.

"There are three people, a dog, and a lion on my road," she said. "Kill the people and the dog. But bring the lion here to my house. He can work for me."

"At once," said the Monkeys. And away they went.

They broke the Tin Man's arms and legs. They took all the straw out of the Scarecrow and threw his clothes up into a tall tree. Then they took the Lion and carried him to a dark cellar under the Witch's house.

But they could not hurt Dorothy and Toto because of the good Witch's kiss. So the Monkeys picked them up

They threw the Scarecrow's clothes up into a tall tree.

very carefully and carried them to the Witch's house. The Witch saw the kiss on Dorothy's face and was afraid. But she did not tell Dorothy that.

"You must work for me in my house now," she said to the child. "All day, and every day. And remember—I am watching you all the time."

Now Dorothy did not know this, but the red shoes were magic. The Witch wanted those shoes very much, but Dorothy never took them off. She took them off when she washed, of course, but the Witch never went near water. She was very, very afraid of water.

Then, one morning, Dorothy's left shoe fell off.

The Witch picked up the shoe at once. "This is *my* shoe now!" she shouted.

"No, it isn't!" shouted Dorothy angrily. "Give it back to me at once!"

"No!" said the Witch. And then she tried to take Dorothy's right shoe too.

Dorothy loved her red shoes, and she was very angry. There was a bucket of water near the door. Dorothy picked up the bucket and threw the water at the Witch. The water hit her in the face, and she cried out, "Help! Help! The water is killing me! The—water—is …"

And then she disappeared! There was only her tall black hat and a long black dress.

Dorothy looked and looked, but the Witch was not there. Dorothy picked up her red shoe and put it on.

"Now, how can I help my friends?" she said. "Can I call the Magic Monkeys?" She picked up the Witch's black hat and looked at it. "Perhaps I must wear this magic hat when I speak." So she put the hat on and called, "Magic Monkeys—come!"

The Monkeys arrived in a second.

"Please can you help my friends?" asked Dorothy.

"Of course," said the Monkeys. "We must always help the wearer of the magic black hat."

They broke open the dark cellar, and the Cowardly Lion came out. "Free at last!" he said. "Thank you!"

Dorothy threw the water at the Witch.

Then the Monkeys found the Scarecrow's clothes and put some new straw in them. The Scarecrow laughed and jumped. "Thank you!" he said.

Next the Monkeys mended the Tin Man and gave him a new oil can. He moved his arms and legs. "I feel wonderful!" he said. "Thank you!"

Dorothy told her friends about the Witch and the water, and they were all very happy. Toto could not speak, but he jumped up and down very happily.

"Now," said Dorothy, "we must go back to the Wizard of Oz. Magic Monkeys—take us to the Emerald City!"

"Don't forget the magic black hat!" said the Tin Man.

The Monkeys carried them up into the sky, and ten minutes later the friends were once again at the big green door of the Emerald City.

The Monkeys carried them up into the sky.

5

THE OLD MAN FROM KANSAS

The little green man opened the door. He gave them all glasses, and then he took them through the city to the Wizard's house. There, in the long green room, the friends waited, and waited … and waited.

After three hours the Scarecrow said, "I'm tired of waiting." He called the green man. "We want to see the Wizard *now*. Or we're going to call the Magic Monkeys. Please tell the Wizard that."

The green man went away to speak to the Wizard through the door. The Wizard knew about the Magic Monkeys, and he was very afraid of them. So he said to the green man, "These people can come and see me at nine o'clock tomorrow morning."

At nine o'clock the green man took the friends to the Wizard's room. They went in and looked all around, but they could not see anybody. Then a voice said, "I am the Wizard of Oz. Who are you, and what do you want?"

"Where are you?" asked Dorothy.

"I am everywhere, but you can't see me. Now answer me—who are you, and what do you want?"

"You know us all," said the Scarecrow. "You said to me, 'Help Dorothy to kill the Witch of the West, and you can have some brains.' Well, the Witch is dead, and now I want my brains."

"And I want my heart," said the Tin Man.

"And I want to be brave," said the Cowardly Lion.

"And I want to go home to Kansas," said Dorothy.

"Is the Witch truly dead?" asked the Voice.

"Yes," said Dorothy. "I threw a bucket of water over her, and she disappeared."

"Very well," said the Voice. "Come again tomorrow. I must think about things first and—"

"No!" said the Tin Man. "I want my heart now!"

"I'm not going to wait another minute!" said the Scarecrow.

"And I'm going to eat you!" the Lion shouted very angrily. Toto was afraid. He jumped away from the Lion and hit a screen near the wall. The screen fell over, and behind it the friends saw an old man with no hair.

The Tin Man looked angry and picked up his ax.

"Who are you?" he said.

"Please don't hurt me!" said the old man, in a quiet little voice. "I'm the Wizard of Oz."

"But the Wizard of Oz is a big head without a body," said Dorothy.

"No, he's a beautiful woman," said the Scarecrow.

"You're wrong," said the Tin Man. "The Wizard of Oz is a big animal with two heads."

The screen fell over.

"No," said the Lion. "The Wizard is a ball of fire."

"You're all wrong," said the old man. "*I* am the Wizard ... Well, I'm not a true wizard. Oh, I know a lot of tricks, but I don't know any true magic. You see, I'm from Kansas too. I went from town to town and did magic tricks. And I went up in a big balloon. The balloon was always on a rope, but one day something went wrong. The rope broke, and the balloon blew away. For a long time the wind carried my balloon across the sky. Then I came down here, in the country of Oz. The people

"The balloon was always on a rope."

34

saw my balloon and said, 'This man is a wizard! He comes out of the sky!' They were afraid of me and wanted to work for me … So they built this city for me, and I called it the Emerald City. Well, emeralds are green, so I made green glasses for everybody. That's why everything in the city looks green."

The Scarecrow took off his glasses. "Oh," he said. "Now I understand. The Emerald City isn't green. It just *looks* green. It's all a trick."

"That's right," said the old man. "Well, all that happened many years ago. I never went out because I was afraid of the two bad Witches. Now they are dead— thanks to you, Dorothy. But I'm very sorry, I don't know any true magic, so I can't help you."

"You're a very bad man," said Dorothy.

"No, my child. I'm a very good man, but I *am* a very bad wizard, that's true."

"What about my brains?" said the Scarecrow.

"You don't *need* brains. You understand things; you can think, you learn quickly. You're very clever."

"I *want* brains," said the Scarecrow.

"Very well," said the old man. "I can give you some brains tomorrow morning."

"What about my heart?" asked the Tin Man.

"You don't *need* a heart," said the old man. "You laugh, you cry, you love, and you feel sorry for people."

The Tin Man looked angry and picked up his ax.

"All right—please don't hurt me!" said the old man. "I can give you a heart tomorrow morning."

"I want to be brave," said the Cowardly Lion.

"But you *are* brave. You do a lot of brave things! No, no—don't eat me! Come here tomorrow morning. I'm going to make you brave."

"What about Toto and me?" asked Dorothy.

"We can go up in my balloon," said the Wizard. "The wind blew us here from Kansas—perhaps it can blow us back to Kansas again."

* * *

The next morning the friends came again to the Wizard's room. The old man was ready. He took a bottle with

"I'm putting your brains in," said the Wizard.

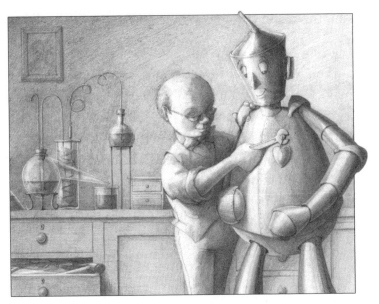

"Wear this always," the Wizard said.

BRAINS on it in big green letters and carefully opened the Scarecrow's head.

"Don't move. I'm putting your brains in," he said. "There—now you're the cleverest scarecrow in Oz." The Scarecrow thanked him.

Next the Wizard gave the Tin Man a small red heart. "Wear this always," he said.

The Tin Man was very happy and thanked the Wizard again and again.

Then the old man took a bottle with BE BRAVE on it. "Drink this," he said to the Cowardly Lion.

The Lion drank. "Yes. Yes, I feel brave!" he shouted. "Very, very brave! Thank you!"

The Wizard smiled at them. "You didn't need my magic," he said. "But you're all happy now, and that's a good thing. Now, Dorothy," he said, "come and see my balloon. It's all ready. I mended it last night."

They went out into the garden behind the Wizard's house. The balloon was very big. There was a small box under it, and the Wizard of Oz jumped into the box.

"Come on, Dorothy!" he shouted. "We're going to Kansas. Say goodbye to your friends."

Dorothy kissed the Scarecrow, the Lion, and the Tin Man, and said goodbye. "Come on, Toto," she said. "We're going home to Kansas. We're going to see Aunt Em and Uncle Henry."

But just then Toto saw a cat. He jumped out of Dorothy's arms and ran after it.

"Toto!" called Dorothy, and she began to run after him.

Toto ran after the cat.

38

6

"EAST, WEST—HOME'S BEST!"

"Leave the dog, and come quickly!" shouted the Wizard. "The rope's going to break!"

Dorothy picked Toto up and ran. "Wait!" she shouted.

But before she got there, the rope *did* break, and the balloon went up, up, up into the sky.

They heard the old man's voice, very far away.

"Ask the Witch of the So–o–o–outh."

But the rope did break …

Then the balloon disappeared. And nobody saw the Wizard of Oz again.

Dorothy began to cry. "Oh, how can I get home now?"

"Put on the magic black hat," said the Scarecrow, "and ask the Magic Monkeys for help. Perhaps they can find the Witch of the South and bring her here."

"Clever Scarecrow!" said Dorothy. She put on the magic hat and called for the Magic Monkeys. When they arrived, she said, "Please find the Witch of the South, and bring her here to the Emerald City."

And five minutes later, a beautiful woman with long red hair arrived. "I am Glinda, the Witch of the South," she said. "What can I do for you, my child?"

"I want to go home to Kansas," said Dorothy. "Please can you help me?"

"Ask your shoes," smiled the good Witch. But Dorothy did not understand.

"Your red shoes," said Glinda, "are magic shoes. They can carry you home. Just close your eyes, and say, 'East, west—home's best.' Then jump."

"Oh, thank you," cried Dorothy happily.

She kissed her friends and said goodbye again. Then she picked up Toto and closed her eyes. "East, west—home's best," she said—and jumped. There was a noise like a wind, and suddenly Dorothy was in the sky. The red shoes fell off her feet, and she never saw them again.

When she opened her eyes, there she was—back in Kansas. And there were Aunt Em and Uncle Henry, in a field by a new little house.

"Dorothy!" cried Aunt Em. She ran and took Dorothy in her arms. "Oh, Dorothy, what happened to you? And where did you come from?"

"From the country of Oz," said Dorothy. "But I'm home again now—and I'm so happy!"

East, west—home's best.

GLOSSARY

blow (past tense **blew**)   to move something through the air

brains   you think with your brains

brave   not afraid of anything

cellar   a room under a building, under the ground

city   a big, important town

clever   quick to learn and understand

clothes   dresses, trousers, shirts, coats, etc.

coward   a person who is afraid of many things

disappear   when something disappears, you can't see it or find it

emerald   a beautiful green jewel

fall (past tense **fell**)   to go down suddenly to a lower place

heart   the part of you which feels, loves, is happy, etc.

hurt   to do bad things to people

magic   when strange, exciting, unusual things happen

mend   to make something good again (e.g., a broken window)

pick up   to take something up in your hand

shout (*v*)   to speak very loudly

strange   if something is strange to you, you do not know it or understand it

tin   a soft white metal

tricks   clever things which look like magic, but which are not magic

voice   you speak, shout, sing, etc. with your voice

witch   a woman in stories who can do magic

wizard   a man in stories who can do magic

The Wizard of Oz

ACTIVITIES

Before Reading

1 Read the story introduction on the first page of the book and the back cover. How much do you know now about the story? Check one box for each sentence.

	YES	NO
1 Dorothy wants to stay in Oz.	☐	☐
2 Dorothy's brother is called Toto.	☐	☐
3 There are four witches in Oz.	☐	☐
4 The Wizard of Oz lives in the Emerald City.	☐	☐
5 Dorothy makes three new friends in Oz.	☐	☐
6 Dorothy's friends are children.	☐	☐
7 The road to the Emerald City is green.	☐	☐

2 What is going to happen in the story? Can you guess? Check one box for each sentence.

	YES	NO
1 The witches are all bad women.	☐	☐
2 The Wizard helps Dorothy and her friends.	☐	☐
3 Dorothy kills someone.	☐	☐
4 The Wizard kills someone.	☐	☐
5 Dorothy goes home to Kansas.	☐	☐
6 Dorothy's friends go to Kansas with her.	☐	☐

ACTIVITIES

While Reading

Read Chapter 1. Choose the correct words for this passage.

Dorothy lived in Kansas with her *mother and father / aunt and uncle*. Sometimes there was *bad weather / a bad animal* called a cyclone. When a cyclone came, people stayed in rooms *on top of / under* their houses. One day a cyclone came and blew *Dorothy and Toto / Aunt Em and Uncle Henry* and the house into the sky. They went to sleep and when they opened their eyes, they were in *Kansas / Oz*. The house fell on the Witch of the *East / North* and killed her, so the people were very *happy / angry*. Dorothy took the Witch's red *shoes / hat*. She wanted to go home, and the good Witch said: "You must ask the *Wizard / Witch* of Oz for help. Follow the *red / yellow* brick road to the Emerald City."

Read Chapter 2, and then match Dorothy's new friends with the sentences.

The Scarecrow / The Tin Man / The Cowardly Lion

1 . . . is made of straw.
2 . . . has no brains.
3 . . . doesn't have a heart.
4 . . . is afraid of fire.
5 . . . has an ax.
6 . . . is afraid of everything.
7 . . . went out in the rain.
8 . . . jumped across the river.
9 . . . cut down a tree.
10 . . . made friends with Toto.

Before you read Chapter 3, can you guess what happens? Choose the best ending for each sentence.

1 The Wizard is . . .
   a) an animal.
   b) a man.
   c) a lot of different things.
2 The Wizard wants to see . . .
   a) Dorothy, but not her friends.
   b) the four friends together.
   c) the four friends one by one.
3 The Wizard tells Dorothy . . .
   a) to kill someone for him.
   b) to get a lot of money for him.
   c) to go away and never come back.

Read Chapter 3, and then answer these questions.

1 What did everybody in the Emerald City wear?
2 What did Dorothy see on the green chair?
3 What did the Scarecrow, the Tin Man, and the Lion see?

Read Chapter 4. Choose the best question-word for these questions, and then answer them.

How / What / Where / Who / Why
1 . . . called the Magic Monkeys to her?
2 . . . many Monkeys were there?

3 . . . did the Monkeys break?
4 . . . did the Monkeys do to the Scarecrow?
5 . . . did the Monkeys take the Lion?
6 . . . couldn't the Monkeys hurt Dorothy and Toto?
7 . . . did the Witch of the West want Dorothy's shoes?
8 . . . did the Witch of the West die?
9 . . . did Dorothy wear to call the Magic Monkeys?
10 . . . did Dorothy and her friends get back to the Emerald City?

Read Chapter 5. Are these sentences true (T) or false (F)? Rewrite the false ones with the correct information.

1 The Wizard was afraid of the green man.
2 The Wizard was a beautiful woman.
3 The Wizard knew a lot of true magic.
4 The Wizard came from Kansas in a balloon.
5 The Emerald City was green.
6 The Wizard gave the Tin Man a heart.
7 Toto ran after a cat.

Before you read Chapter 6, can you guess what happens? Check one box for each sentence.

	YES	NO
1 The Wizard disappears in the balloon.	☐	☐
2 Dorothy and Toto get back into the balloon.	☐	☐
3 Dorothy meets another witch.	☐	☐
4 The Magic Monkeys help Dorothy again.	☐	☐

47

After Reading

1 **What did Dorothy try to tell Aunt Em about Oz? Write out their conversation in the correct order and put in the speakers' names. Aunt Em speaks first (number 3).**

1 _____ "Oz? Where's that? Is it in Kansas?"

2 _____ "A magic country? Are you feeling all right?"

3 _____ "What happened to you, Dorothy? Where were you?"

4 _____ "Magic shoes? But you aren't wearing any shoes!"

5 _____ "I'm OK, really I am. I made some wonderful new friends in Oz. They helped me a lot."

6 _____ "I was in Oz."

7 _____ "No, it's a magic country, a long way from here."

8 _____ "No, they couldn't come with me. My magic shoes carried me."

9 _____ "Oh! How strange. Perhaps they fell off."

10 _____ "That's nice. Where are your friends now? Did they bring you home?"

2 **Find words from the story to complete the sentences and then the crossword (all words go across). Now can you find the eighth word going down?**

1 The Monkeys put the Lion in the _____.

2 The _____ helped the wearer of the black hat.

3 The friends saw the Wizard when the _____ fell over.
4 The Wizard could do _____, but not true magic.
5 The Wizard came to Oz in a _____.
6 The road to the city was made of _____ bricks.
7 The old man was a good man, but a bad _____.

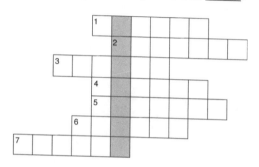

3 **Dorothy told Aunt Em about her friends, but when Aunt Em told Uncle Henry, she got a lot of things wrong. Can you find her mistakes and correct them?**

"Dorothy met a scarecrow made of tin. He could eat and drink, but he couldn't talk. He had no heart, so he couldn't think. Then she met a man made of straw. He couldn't see because he went out in the rain. So Dorothy got some glasses and helped him. But he wasn't happy because he had no brains. Then she met a lion. He was very brave, and often hurt people. They went to see the Wizard of Oz together. When they came to a very big river, the scarecrow cut down a tree with his pole, and they all walked across it."

4 Here is a new illustration for the story. Find the best place in the story to put the picture, and answer these questions.

The picture goes on page ____.

1 Who is wearing the magic hat, and why?

2 Who is coming out of the cellar?

3 What are the Monkeys going to do next?

Now write a caption for the illustration.

Caption: _____

5 **The Scarecrow, the Tin Man, and the Lion didn't need the Wizard's help. Why not? Complete these sentences and then answer the question.**

1 He thought of cutting down a _____ to cross the _____.
2 He didn't want to _____ animals, because he felt _____ for them.
3 He was _____ of falling, but he _____ across a river.

So who was brave, who was clever, and who had a heart?

6 **Now say what you think. Answer these questions.**

1 Is it better to have brains, to have a heart, or to be brave?
2 The Wizard said, "You didn't need my magic. But you're all happy now, and that's a good thing." Was he right?
3 Imagine that you can ask the Wizard for help. What are you going to ask for?

7 **What did you think about the people and animals in this story? Choose some names and complete these sentences. Use as many words as you like.**

Dorothy / the Wizard of Oz / the Scarecrow / the Lion / the Tin Man / the Magic Monkeys / the Witch of the North

1 I liked _____ because _____.
2 I didn't like _____ because _____.
3 I felt sorry for _____ because/when _____.
4 I was angry with _____ because/when _____.

ABOUT THE AUTHOR

Lyman Frank Baum was born in Chittenago, New York, in 1856. He came from a rich family; his father made his money in the oil business and also had a theater. Baum could not play games when he was a child because he had a bad heart, so he read a lot of story books.

His first job was as an actor, but he also wrote for newspapers and for the theater. In 1882, he got married and soon had two sons. He needed to make money for his family, so he went to work in his father's business. After his father died, Baum and his family moved to South Dakota and opened a shop. But it closed after two years, and Baum moved to Chicago and began to work as a writer again.

Baum now had four sons, and he liked to tell them stories, so in 1897 he wrote his first children's book. He was soon very successful, and in 1900 *The Wonderful Wizard of Oz* came out. It was just a bedtime story for his sons, and it was not very well written, but it was, and still is, a very famous book. Oz was the first really good "magic world" in books for American children. Some people said that the Wizard was like Baum himself.

Baum wrote many more Oz books and also made some short films. In 1911 he moved to Hollywood, but sadly he lost all his money. He still wrote one book every year, but he was very ill and died in 1919. After he died, other people wrote books about Oz, and a very famous film was made by MGM in 1939, with Judy Garland as Dorothy.

OXFORD BOOKWORMS LIBRARY

Classics • Crime & Mystery • Factfiles • Fantasy & Horror
Human Interest • Playscripts • Thriller & Adventure
True Stories • World Stories

The OXFORD BOOKWORMS LIBRARY provides enjoyable reading in English, with a wide range of classic and modern fiction, non-fiction, and plays. It includes original and adapted texts in seven carefully graded language stages which take learners from beginner to advanced level.

All Stage 1 titles, as well as over eighty other titles from Starter to Stage 6, are available as audio recordings. All Starters and many titles at Stages 1 to 4 are specially recommended for younger learners. Every Bookworm is illustrated, and Starters and Factfiles have full-color illustrations.

The OXFORD BOOKWORMS LIBRARY also offers extensive support. Each book contains an introduction to the story, notes about the author, a glossary, and activities. Additional resources include tests and worksheets, as well as answers for these and for the activities in the books. There is advice on running a class library, using audio recordings, and the many ways of using Oxford Bookworms in reading programs. Resource materials are available on the website <www.oup.com/elt/gradedreaders>.

The *Oxford Bookworms Collection* is a series for advanced learners. It consists of volumes of short stories by well-known authors, both classic and modern. Texts are not abridged or adapted in any way, but carefully selected to be accessible to the advanced student.

You can find details and a full list of titles in the *Oxford Bookworms Library Catalog* and *Oxford English Language Teaching Catalogs*, and on the website <www.oup.com/elt/gradedreaders>.

The Adventures of Tom Sawyer

MARK TWAIN

Retold by Nick Bullard

Tom Sawyer does not like school. He does not like work, and he never wants to get out of bed in the morning. But he likes swimming, fishing, and having adventures with his friends. And he has a lot of adventures. One night, he and his friend Huck Finn go to the graveyard to look for ghosts.

They don't see any ghosts that night. They see something worse than a ghost—much, much worse ...

The Phantom of the Opera

JENNIFER BASSETT

It is 1880 in the Opera House in Paris. Everybody is talking about the Phantom of the Opera, the ghost that lives somewhere under the Opera House. The Phantom is a man in black clothes. He is a body without a head; he is a head without a body. He has a yellow face, he has no nose, and he has black holes for eyes. Everybody is afraid of the Phantom—the singers, the dancers, the directors, the stage workers ...

But who has actually seen him?

The Elephant Man

TIM VICARY

He is not beautiful. His mother does not want him, and children run away from him. People laugh at him and call him "The Elephant Man."

Then someone speaks to him—and listens to him! At the age of 27, Joseph Merrick finds a friend for the first time in his life.

This is a true and tragic story. It is also a famous film.

Pocahontas

TIM VICARY

A beautiful young Indian girl and a brave Englishman. Black eyes and blue eyes. A friendly smile, a laugh, a look of love ... But this is North America in 1607, and love is not easy. The girl is the daughter of King Powhatan, and the Englishman is a white man. And the Indians of Virginia do not want the white men in their beautiful country.

This is the famous story of Pocahontas and her love for the Englishman John Smith.

Huckleberry Finn

MARK TWAIN

Retold by Diane Mowat

Who wants to live in a house, wear clean clothes, be good, and go to school every day? Not young Huckleberry Finn, that's for sure.

So Huck runs away and is soon floating down the great Mississippi River on a raft. With him is Jim, a black slave who is also running away. But life is not always easy for the two friends.

And there's 300 dollars waiting for anyone who catches poor Jim …

BOOKWORMS · CLASSICS · STAGE 2

Robinson Crusoe

DANIEL DEFOE

Retold by Diane Mowat

"I often walked along the shore, and one day I saw something in the sand. I went over to look at it more carefully … It was a footprint—the footprint of a man!"

In 1659 Robinson Crusoe was shipwrecked on a small island off the coast of South America. After fifteen years alone, he suddenly learns that there is another person on the island. But will this man be a friend—or an enemy?